# Mice to the Rescue!

## Michelle V. Dionetti

little rainbow

**Troll Associates**

Published by Troll Associates, Inc. Little Rainbow is a trademark of
Troll Associates.

Printed in the United States of America.

10   9   8   7   6   5   4   3   2   1


Library of Congress Cataloging-in-Publication Data

Dionetti, Michelle, (date)
    Mice to the rescue! / by Michelle V. Dionetti; illustrated by Carol
Newsom.
        p.   cm.
    Summary: A family of mice living in a fabric shop joins forces with
their mouse neighbors to protect the store from a human with evil
intentions.
    ISBN 0-8167-3515-8 (pbk.)     0-8167-3712-6 (lib.)
    [1. Mice—Fiction.]     I. Newsom, Carol, ill.     II. Title.
PZ7.D6214Mi     1995
[FIC]—dc20                                        94-23641

# CAST OF CHARACTERS

**THE CALICOS**

> **MILES:** the provider and worrier
>
> **FLO:** his wife, who likes her privacy
>
> **SKIPPER:** their son, who likes secrets and knows more than he tells
>
> **MISSY:** their daughter, who makes no secret of her curiosity

**MR. MAX:** the villain; proprietor of The Gray Cat Inn

**MISSES FINCH AND FINICKY:** the fussy operators of The Calico Scrapbag, the fabric shop where the Calicos make their home.

**THE SQUEALERS**

> **FATTY:** whose greed leads to disaster at the inn
>
> **LETITIA:** whose generosity helps save the day
>
> **GLADYS:** Missy's first friend, who is good-natured and can read

**AND:** all the other mice who make up the mouse community of The Gray Cat Inn, and whose bravery makes victory possible

# TABLE OF CONTENTS

# CHAPTER

On the day the trouble began, neither Miss Finch nor Miss Finicky, the owners of the fabric shop called The Calico Scrapbag, nor Mr. Max, owner of The Gray Cat Inn next door, had any inkling that their lives were about to be shaped by a family of mice.

At the inn, amid the usual dinnertime bustle, Mr. Max stood beside the kitchen window and scowled through his oily mustache at The Calico Scrapbag.

"Fabric shop, indeed!" he muttered blackly, rubbing his fingers together. "It should be a parking lot! I'd love to pour hot sauce on the silly thing and feed it to the city dump!"

Meanwhile, it was closing time at The Calico Scrapbag. Miss Finicky was, as usual, bustling around the shop rearranging things, and Miss Finch was, as usual, stalking around after her, straightening them up again.

Under the cutting table in the center of the shop, there were three deep shelves. At the back of the very bottom shelf, behind some bolts of lining, was a mouse hole. And behind the mouse hole door lived a family of mice. They called themselves the Calicos.

The day the trouble began, Missy Calico stirred and sat up in her canopy bed. She awakened every day at 5:00 P.M. with the striking of the clock in the shop, which signaled closing time.

Missy sat still for a moment, listening. In the next room, her brother, Skipper, was probably already dressed, impatient to be up and hunting. Skip was a collector. He loved to look for treasures to store in his secret hiding place. Across the hall, their father, Miles, was undoubtedly sitting on the edge of the bed, anxious to get breakfast started. And their mother, Flo, was certainly still in bed, content to relax until the last possible moment.

Missy bounced up and down on her bed, tired of sitting still. She listened to the familiar shop-closing noises as Misses Finch and Finicky shut the drawers and swept the floors and locked the doors.

But what was this? A knock at the back door of The Calico Scrapbag? Missy bounced out of bed. She tiptoed to the mouse hole entrance, where the listening was better. Miles was already there, watchful and anxious. Flo wandered out, and Skipper finally joined them, looking bored. Together, they listened as Miss Finch opened the back door of the shop.

"Good evening," said an oily voice.

"Mr. Max!" exclaimed Missy.

She was immediately silenced by a frown from Flo, a shush from Miles, and a dig in the ribs from Skip.

"Well, ladies," continued Mr. Max. "How are we today?"

"*We* are fine," said Miss Finch. "What can we do for *you*? New curtains or tablecloths, perhaps?"

"Ah, no." Mr. Max's voice shuddered slightly. "Mine are custom-made in New York, of course. But I *did* wonder, ladies, if you might be interested in selling your business? For a very satisfactory sum, naturally."

Misses Finch and Finicky gave astonished gasps. In the mouse hole, Miles took out his monogrammed handkerchief and mopped his brow. Flo put a paw to her heart. Missy frowned in bewilderment, and Skipper just shrugged.

"I wouldn't think of selling," said Miss Finch firmly. "I started this business thirty years ago, and here I intend to say. This business," said Miss Finch grandly, "is my life!"

Miles and Flo exchanged a glance of relief.

"I am sorry to hear that," said Mr. Max ominously. "But—perhaps you will change your minds. Good evening, ladies."

The back door shut with a muffled bang. Misses Finch and Finicky stood silent. A long minute passed before anyone spoke.

"The idea!" said Miss Finicky in amazement.

"Such nonsense!" said Miss Finch sharply.

There was a babble and a flurry while they closed the shop. For once, Miss Finicky didn't fuss over the buttons. For once, Miss Finch didn't close her workbasket just so and hang it by the back door. As soon as the door closed and the key turned in the lock, the Calicos came alive.

"Sell the shop!" muttered Flo as she placed a pin-box lid of bread crumbs and raisins on the kitchen table. "What on earth could Max want with it?"

"Doesn't matter. He'll never get it," declared

Miles in a warlike tone.

"Would we have to move?" asked Missy.

Miles tapped the table nervously.

"I will *not* move back to The Gray Cat Inn," declared Flo in her that-settles-it voice, and Missy felt a little better.

Skipper looked agitated. Missy supposed he was wondering how he would move his secret hoard, and where. She thought of all her own treasures and began to worry again.

"Can I bring my canopy bed?" she asked.

"There won't be any need," said Miles loudly. "We are staying right here."

"But what if they sell?" demanded Missy.

"They won't sell," said Flo firmly. "This store is Miss Finch's life, isn't it? You heard her. They've been working here for thirty years. And it's as much *our* home as theirs, isn't it? We won't let them sell, and that's that."

"How will we stop them?" demanded Missy.

"Probably we won't have to do a thing," said Miles.

Skipper stirred. "If that Max messes around with us, there are ways to get back at him," he said with a glare.

Everyone stared at him, wondering what in the world he could mean.

"Well, we won't borrow trouble," said Flo, putting an end to the conversation.

"Can I go to the inn for food with you tonight, Father?" asked Skip, dipping a bread crumb into a thimbleful of jelly.

"To be sure," said Miles.

"I want to go, too," said Missy.

"Well, you can't, Miss," said Miles sharply. "You'll help your mother stitch the new slipcover for the sofa."

"Why can't I ever go outside?" cried Missy. "It's because I'm a girl!"

"It's because you're too careless. Being a girl has nothing to do with it," said Miles. "Remember last month, when you stopped in the driveway to stare at the stars?"

"I won't do that again," pleaded Missy.

"You have the run of the shop, and that's enough," said Flo. "Come now. Finish your breakfast. We have to get the brocade for the new slipcover while it's still light."

# CHAPTER 2

The best time for family outings was immediately after breakfast, when there was still outside light in the shop. Each Calico had a sturdy carrying case of his or her own design for gathering things. Skipper's was a large canvas knapsack, which he strapped securely onto his back. Missy's was a rather over-embroidered shoulder bag, too large to be graceful, but roomy enough for all the beads and sequins she loved to gather. Flo had a shopping bag made of upholstery fabric, and Miles had a canvas knapsack like Skip's and a drawstring duffle bag, as well.

Tonight, before Skipper and Missy could go exploring, they had to help Miles and Flo cut a length of red brocade. This involved dragging the smallest pair of scissors from the cutting table to the bolt of red brocade, stretching the cloth straight, and working the scissors to cut it. Once that task was accomplished, Skipper swung down from the shelf of brocades and disappeared, probably off to his hoard.

Missy toyed with the idea of following him, as she sometimes did to try to discover his hiding place, but she didn't feel like it. Instead, she explored the wastebasket. A quick look rewarded her with a two-inch piece of blue lace. Missy happily tucked it into her shoulder bag. Then she climbed up the cutting table and went in search of sequins.

The cutting table was Missy's favorite place. There were endless spools of ribbon and bags of beads and sequins hanging on the post behind it. Missy dropped her shoulder bag in the middle of the table and hurried to investigate the section where the sequins were displayed. Row upon glittering row stretched up out of sight. Missy debated whether or not to attempt climbing to the bag of pink sequins three hooks up; chancy. She had just begun to climb when she heard a noise.

There was a thump, then a scrape. Then a scratchy sound from the back door, and a mutter, and a kind of gentle tugging. Missy didn't have time to run home. Quickly, she sped across the cutting table and into Miss Finicky's open workbasket.

There was another thump, louder this time, and a slow creak as the back door opened. Missy peered over the edge of the workbasket. A beam of light shone in, and Missy sank back into the workbasket—directly onto a pincushion.

"Ulp!" she squeaked.

The flashlight beam stopped moving. Missy's paw flew to cover her mouth, and her heart beat so hard she thought the intruder might hear it. But after a moment the beam of light began to move again. A huge black form entered the shop. Missy crinkled her sensitive nose. She could smell onions and roast beef and antipasto and blue cheese. Mr. Max! What was he doing in the shop?

The light from Mr. Max's flashlight played across the cutting table. It moved over the workbasket. Missy closed her eyes tightly, thinking that if she couldn't see him, he couldn't see her. The light moved on.

Suddenly, Mr. Max uttered an exclamation and set the flashlight down.

"What's this?" he said under his breath.

Missy's heart stopped. Did he see Skipper? Was Father out looking for her? Cautiously, she peeked.

Mr. Max was holding the little shoulder bag in his hand, turning it over to look at the embroidery.

"Astonishing," he murmured. "I do believe the old biddies play with dolls!"

Chuckling, he threw Missy's shoulder bag down and picked up the flashlight. Missy watched curiously. Where was he going? He seemed to be interested in the front counter, where the cash register was. He was fiddling with the locks and opening drawers. The nerve of him! Missy thought. Stealing from old ladies!

Mr. Max put his hand into his pocket and pulled out a small can. He approached the front window. Missy heard a hissing sound and smelled a strong odor. The awful smell made her want to choke. What was he doing, anyway?

Suddenly, Mr. Max spun around and looked straight at the workbasket, or so it seemed to Missy. What could she do? She fainted.

# CHAPTER

3

When Missy came to, she was lying on the sofa in the parlor. She was covered with a red afghan that Flo had knitted, and water was being poured over her head. Missy sat up, sputtering. "Stop that!" she said.

Skipper kept pouring.

"Stop!"

Skipper stopped.

"You've finally woken up, I see," said Flo.

"Where's my shoulder bag?" demanded Missy.

"On the kitchen table," said Flo sharply, "and no thanks to you. Imagine leaving it out on the cutting table in plain sight!"

"I know," groaned Missy.

"He picked it up," spat Flo. "It smells like antipasto."

"He thought it was a doll's purse," offered Skipper.

"How do you know?" asked Flo.

"I was in the cottons across from the cutting table when he came in," said Skip.

Missy stood up and tried to brush the water off her head. Flo handed her a piece of toweling.

"What was he doing, anyway?" asked Missy.

"He was messing about with paint," said Miles, who had come in and was hanging his sweater on the hook by the door. "Awful smell, paint has."

"What was he painting?" asked Flo.

"He was painting the windows." Miles sat down and tapped his foot nervously. "I think he wrote something on the windows in black paint."

"Dirty human!" hissed Flo.

"I wish there were some way of washing the windows before the ladies arrive in the morning," said Miles. "It will scare them half to death."

"Vandal!" exclaimed Flo. She took two long, deep breaths and returned to matters at hand. "But we're not getting the sofa done. Get up, Missy, and hold the brocade so I can cut the pattern."

"Ugh," said Missy. "I feel faint."

"None of that nonsense," said Flo. "It will train your mind to be less flighty. Fainting dead away!"

Missy sighed.

"How'd I get home?" she asked.

"I brought you," said Skipper importantly.

"Oh," said Missy. "Thanks."

"You're my only sister," said Skip as an explanation.

He followed Missy out of the parlor and along a narrow hall to the sewing room.

"Want this?" he asked casually, as he pulled a plastic ballerina charm from behind his back. It was the sort of charm that came from gumball machines.

"Oh," breathed Missy. "It's lovely!"

Skipper pushed the charm into Missy's paws, then turned and escaped down the hall before Flo could ask him to hold the brocade, too.

"Hurry up, Miss," scolded Flo.

"Look what Skipper gave me!" exclaimed Missy.

"Humph," said Flo, eyeing the charm sharply. "Fell out of some nasty human child's pocket, I expect."

Missy propped the charm out of sight behind the spool rack, feeling guilty. She didn't want to get Skip into trouble.

"Hold the edge straight," said Flo.

Missy patiently held the cloth while Flo wielded the scissors. Missy loved the sewing room. There was a rocking chair, a spool rack, and a porcelain thimble filled with mouse-sized needles that Miles had patiently filed. A wall of shelves held neatly folded pieces of fabric salvaged from the shop's wastebaskets, and there was a special section for the paper patterns Flo had made.

The new sofa stood in the middle of the room, waiting for its slipcover. Miles had made the sofa from foam rubber. It was to be part of the furnishings of the new music room that Miles and Skipper were building. Miles had taken to making stringed instruments out of odds and ends of wood and strings and wires. He had tried a few drums, made of thimbles and bottle caps stretched with pieces of leather, too. Missy could hardly wait for the music room to be completed. It would be so elegant. The sofa would be covered in red brocade. Missy would sit on it in her pink velvet cape—her favorite scrap—and pretend to be Queen.

"I don't like that human, Max," said Flo suddenly.

Missy shivered. "Me neither!" she said.

"I hate to think what it will be like in the morning when those two poor ladies see that paint!"

"Can I stay put and listen?" asked Missy.

"No."

"Please!"

"You need your sleep."

"I could sleep now and get up at bedtime," begged Missy.

Flo paused for a moment, considering. She shot Missy an alert glance out of bright black eyes.

"Guess you're old enough," she said. "You'll be quiet?"

"Yes," said Missy.

"All right, then," said Flo. "See that your father and Skipper have their knapsacks ready for tonight's trip, and then you can go to bed."

Missy tied a scrap of the red brocade onto her tail and hurried off to the kitchen. She found Skipper eating a piece of cheese and arguing with Miles about food.

"Too dangerous," Miles was saying. "Max will be all keyed up after breaking in and painting windows. Better stick to the usual."

"He'll be too keyed up to notice us," insisted Skipper. "It's just the night to try the garbage cans for fresh pastry."

"We'll see how it goes," said Miles.

Missy pulled over the knapsacks.

"I'm going to take a nap," she announced, "and then get up at eight o'clock in the morning to hear all the commotion in the shop."

"Ho, ho!" laughed Skip. "Bows on her tail, and she wants to sit up with the grown-ups!"

"Mother said I could, so there!" cried Missy.

"Stop arguing," said Miles. "Come, Skipper, time to go. The inn's closing."

Missy followed them through a mouse hole in their kitchen and down a long passageway between the inside and outside walls. They went past a tricky bit of electrical wiring, then out of a crack in the wall that overlooked the grass next to the shop.

"Have a good haul," whispered Missy from the crack.

"Watch out for the wires going back," Miles told her.

Missy watched him and Skipper disappear into the grass shadows.

# CHAPTER

4

The way into the inn was almost directly across the driveway. There was a hidden opening just next to the outside faucet. Skipper and Miles pushed through this opening easily. Then it was a question of keeping between the walls as they traveled around the back of the building to the inn's kitchen. Except for a tangle of pipes, which were sometimes hot, and the wiring, it was quite an easy route. The mouse hole came out very conveniently behind the great refrigerator, so they were safely hidden from view.

"I smell apple pie," said Skipper, wrinkling his long nose.

"Fresh," said Miles, licking his whiskers.

He crept from behind the refrigerator and looked cautiously about.

"Trouble," he whispered, coming back to Skipper. "Fatty Squealer."

"Ugh," said Skip.

Fatty Squealer lived with his family under the corner cupboard in the kitchen. It was dangerous to gather food with him because he was too greedy to be careful.

"Just what we need," murmured Miles. "I wish he'd waited till later. I'm nervous enough as it is."

"Kitchen's quiet," whispered Skipper. "You could watch Fatty, and I could try the pantry for some cereal or rice. I'm tired of dried peas."

Miles mopped his brow with his monogrammed handkerchief.

"Can you do it alone?" he asked. "You know the way? And no noise?"

"Been there often enough, haven't I?" said Skipper. "You worry too much, Father," he added.

"Well," said Miles, sighing at the truth of his words, "all right. But if there's danger, you freeze and then duck under the sink—there are those holes behind the pipes."

"Yes, sir," said Skip patiently. "I know. We drill once a week, remember?"

Miles sighed. He watched Skipper creep to the side of the refrigerator. Finding the coast clear, Skipper scooted across the narrow space between the refrigerator and the cupboards. Then he vanished into the cupboards themselves, where he would take a hidden passageway into the pantry. Miles turned his attention to Fatty.

Fatty Squealer started across the garbage bin. Miles watched him anxiously. Garbage work was dangerous. You never knew what you'd find, diving into a mountain of odds and ends, and climbing out again was hazardous—but exciting. Miles thought that it should never be done alone. But Fatty always hunted alone—so that he could stuff his face in private, it was said. Miles didn't care what Fatty ate on the spot. But Fatty didn't seem to understand how much his hunting alone worried his family and friends.

Miles watched Fatty appear briefly in the space between the oven and the bin containing the garbage cans. After Fatty disappeared, there was a pause, then a scrabbling noise, and then silence. Miles waited and listened for a long time. Just as he began to wonder whether Fatty needed rescuing, Skipper puffed triumphantly up behind him, bearing a bulging knapsack.

"Grape-Nuts," he whispered smugly.

"Good, son, good," said Miles. "You stay here, Skip. I'm just going behind the garbage cans to see if Fatty's loaded himself down too much to climb up again."

"Oh, you know Fatty," said Skipper. "He's probably just eating as he goes."

Miles set out on the dangerous passage from the refrigerator to the garbage bin. But he'd barely taken a few steps when he heard footsteps in the hall. He streaked back behind the refrigerator.

"Into the hole, Skipper, just in case," he ordered.

Skipper moved back. There was another footstep, and the sound of a human clearing his throat.

"That's Max!" exclaimed Skipper.

"Shush!" ordered Miles.

Fatty chose this moment to come out from behind the garbage bin. He was pulling an extremely full bag and on his face was a blissful smile.

"The fool!" muttered Miles.

Fatty was between the garbage bin and the oven when Mr. Max swung open the kitchen door. Light fell across the polished floor, catching Fatty in plain sight. Fatty squealed.

"A mouse! A mouse in my kitchen!" cried Mr. Max.

At the sound of Mr. Max's voice, Fatty jumped for cover. But he kept hold of his heavy bag, which made it slow going.

"Idiot!" whispered Miles.

When caught, a mouse should drop everything and run, and the last place he or she should run is home. Before you knew it, there would be a trap at the front door, and a mound of poison.

"Out!" roared Mr. Max, mustache trembling.

He picked up a broom and jabbed it at Fatty. Fatty yelped. Then he squeezed between Mr. Max's feet, raced in front of the oven, and scurried straight under the corner cupboard to his front door.

"Oh, no!" groaned Skipper.

"Lost his head," muttered Miles. "Lost his head entirely. It's a tragedy for his family."

Mr. Max had dropped to his bony knees and was shoving the broom under the corner cupboard.

"Traps!" he shouted when at last he got to his feet. "Poison! Mice in my kitchen!"

"It's a crisis," whispered Miles.

"Cats!" shouted Mr. Max.

Even Skipper began to sweat.

"*Gray* cats!" Mr. Max went on. "*Two* gray cats!"

Mr. Max threw down the broom and swept his arms wide. "And may they have many little gray kittens!" he shouted triumphantly.

Miles sadly shook his head. He motioned to Skipper, and they crawled quietly back through the mouse hole.

"Cats," whispered Skipper. "This is terrible." He was very frightened.

Miles didn't know what to do. First the shop was threatened, and now the inn. Were the Calicos going to lose their happy life? Would they be forced to move?

"I won't have it!" said Miles. "I won't have it at all!"

# CHAPTER

5

Missy rolled over and yawned.

"Wake up, Lazytail," said Flo impatiently, shaking Missy's shoulder. "You've got to be settled before the shop's open. Besides, there's news. Come *on!*"

Missy rolled away from Flo and out of bed. She yawned again, shaking herself awake. It was odd to be waking up when she was used to going to sleep. She started to tie a piece of pink lace around her tail.

"Don't fuss now," said Flo sharply. "Come into the hall, and bring your pillow with you for sitting. And wear stockings so you won't make any sound."

After covering her feet, Missy padded after Flo. Miles and Skipper were already in the hall, and Skip was gnawing on one of the Grape-Nuts he'd brought back from the inn.

"Oh, Grape-Nuts!" Missy exclaimed.

Miles turned and scowled at them.

"No more of that chewing, Skipper," he said. "Sit down, Missy, and be still. We need to keep our heads. First this trouble in the shop, and now the inn!"

"What trouble?" demanded Missy.

"Fatty Squealer was almost caught last night," said Skipper. "I saw him."

"Caught!" exclaimed Missy.

"Mr. Max is thinking of getting a cat," said Miles nervously. "*Two* cats."

"*Gray* cats," added Skip.

There was an awful silence while everyone thought about cats. Missy felt her heart squeeze. Cats were horrible creatures. They were prehistoric, she believed, like dinosaurs, only covered in fur. Cats liked to hunt mice.

"We won't be safe, will we?" asked Missy slowly. It wasn't really a question.

"No," said Miles.

Missy shivered miserably. Big furry tails and sharp teeth and dragon claws . . .

The clock in the shop began to count the hour. There was a scrape at the back door.

"Quiet now," warned Flo.

The Calicos were very still. They listened to the clock strike 8:00 A.M. Upstairs, the door flew open with a bang.

"The nerve!" said Miss Finch furiously. "Written right on our front window! In black paint! On the inside!" She gasped. "Does some horrible person have a key to my shop?"

Instead of going straight to the broom closet for rags and mops and window cleaner, Miss Finch marched to the telephone and dialed a number.

"The police, please," came Miss Finch's voice. "I'll have to leave the paint where it is until the police see it," she said to herself. "Hello, police? I would like to report a crime!"

Miss Finch gave the address and hung up. "Disgraceful!" she said crisply. She began to straighten the bolts of fabric and dust the shelves with more than her usual vigor.

"What's going on?" wailed a voice. "'Ladies Beware!' written all over the windows! It's dreadful, just dreadful!"

Miss Finicky hurried into the shop through the back door.

"And your workbasket, too! Didn't you hang it up last night? Oh, dear, was anything taken?"

"Just a swatch of brocade, of all things. Though I suppose a customer may have cut a sample sometime yesterday," replied Miss Finch.

"Oh!" gasped Miss Finicky, rushing around the shop in agitation. "Oh, dear, we shall have to change the locks!"

"After the police have been here," said Miss Finch.

"Police!" exclaimed Miss Finicky. "You shouldn't have dusted, dear; fingerprints, you know."

Miss Finch groaned.

"You're right. But I haven't finished," she said. "I haven't dusted the counter yet, or the cutting table. Or the back door."

The Calicos stayed completely still as they listened to the ladies talk. Soon the police arrived. So did the locksmith, some news reporters, and quite a few early customers. Miss Finicky went out to buy paint remover and then scrubbed the window. Missy listened to all of these proceedings with great concentration, but she heard nothing at all that indicated the ladies even suspected Mr. Max. The thunderous roar of the vacuum cleaner

finally began, and the Calicos were free to whisper.

"Why do you suppose he did it?" Missy whispered into Skipper's ear.

"To frighten them into selling," Skip replied.

"I don't think it's working," Missy whispered back.

"I have a headache," whispered Miles fretfully. "I'm going to bed."

He pulled his silk bathrobe tight around him and crept away to the blue-and-white bedroom. After a moment, Skipper also headed off.

"Go on, then, Miss!" said Flo firmly. "I am very tired, and I want you safely in your room before I go to bed."

"All right," said Missy reluctantly.

She padded back to her room. There she gathered up an armful of the dolls she and Flo had made—mouse dolls, of course, with little nightgowns and bonnets and aprons and ribbony dresses—and took them to bed. The roar of the vacuum stopped. For a long time, Missy sat in silence, listening to unfamiliar daytime noises and wondering about cats, before she finally dropped off to sleep.

# CHAPTER

6

The Calicos sat around their kitchen table, which was really a large, empty ribbon spool, looking every bit as glum as they felt.

"What can we do against cats?" worried Miles.

"We haven't got cats to worry about yet," said Flo sensibly. "We've got to solve the shop problem first."

"The way I look at it," said Miles, leaning over the red-checked tablecloth, "if Mr. Max could paint windows, he might do worse."

"What do you mean?" demanded Flo.

"He might do damage to the inside of the shop," said Miles, "like cutting cloth into shreds or throwing goods about."

"Oh, nonsense," said Flo.

"Or fire," added Miles impressively.

Missy squealed.

"You're borrowing trouble," said Flo sharply.

"Nasty, evil man!" said Missy.

"But what can we do?" asked Skipper.

"Keep watch," said Miles. "Perhaps we can push things over when Mr. Max least expects a noise. And if there's a fire or something, perhaps we can push the phone off the hook and dial the fire department."

"We could spend the night in the shop," suggested Skipper, "keeping watch."

Missy gave a little hop.

"Good idea, Skipper," Miles said approvingly. "We'll all have different posts. You, Skip, take the front door. If someone tries to come in, you'll have to think of some way to distract him. You, Missy, take the cutting table. You can keep an eye on the back door and signal if anything's wrong."

"She shouldn't be out all night," objected Flo. "She's too young. It's too dangerous."

"She stayed well enough hidden last time," said Miles. "You, Flo, take the middle of the shop."

"I will," said Flo, "as long as I can see my own front door."

"I'll take the counter with the cash register and the phone," announced Miles. "Eat up, now. We won't come home till dawn."

The Calicos finished breakfast in a hurry, then scattered to make preparations for the night's adventure. Missy packed her shoulder bag with every necessity she could think of: a few Grape-Nuts, a plump, sticky raisin packed in foil, and the baby doll who needed a new bonnet. The work would keep her busy, and, besides, she needed someone to talk to if she was expected to stay awake until 8:00 A.M.

Missy met her family at the mouse hole door. Together, they cautiously crept into the shop.

"Looks safe," said Miles softly. "Haven't heard a sound. We'll go out one by one to be sure."

He scooted off toward the front of the shop.

"Don't leave your shoulder bag about tonight," Flo warned Missy.

Missy scampered out without answering. She climbed up the cutting table and settled herself behind a spool of pink, flowered ribbon. The spool was big enough to hide her, and she could crawl inside the hole in the middle of it if she had to. She pulled her baby mouse doll out of her shoulder bag and set about the important business of selecting bonnet material. She soon chose a spool of wide, white lace and patiently began to work a piece off with her teeth.

Meanwhile, Skipper examined the front door's keyhole, planning how to plug it up.

"I must have something put away," he mused.

He ducked quickly into his hiding place when Miles wasn't looking and emerged with erasers and a bit of gum. It was a struggle to push the gum into the keyhole while holding onto the door latch and then to wedge an eraser under the door latch, but Skipper was proud of his work when he'd finished.

"Good idea, Skip," Miles said from below him. "Want to do the same for the back?" Miles carefully did not ask where Skipper had obtained his materials.

"All right," said Skipper. He gathered the rest of the erasers and a piece of dressmaker's chalk from his knapsack and trotted off to the back. Missy peered at him from the cutting board.

"What are you doing?" she called.

"Plugging up the keyholes."

"Come up and see me."

"Can't."

Missy sighed. It was going to be a long night.

Suddenly, there were footsteps outside the shop. Flo whisked home to guard the mouse hole.

Miles squeezed into the space under the telephone receiver. Skipper flew into his hiding place. Missy grabbed her shoulder bag and her baby doll and scrambled into the hole in the spool.

There was a musical sort of crash as a windowpane splintered to the floor. Missy peered out in time to see a hand reach in and unlock the window. With a creak, the window shot up. First a foot with a shiny black boot appeared. Then a skinny black leg. Then, with difficulty, a skinny black back, followed by a skinny black hat. Mr. Max half fell backward into the shop, knocking over a display of buttons.

The buttons fell to the floor, spilling in all directions. Missy wiggled happily. What a good treasure hunt they'd have when Mr. Max had gone!

But Missy wiggled a bit too hard. The spool began to roll toward the end of the cutting table. Oh, no! Missy shut her eyes.

"I mustn't make a sound!" she thought.

The spool came to the edge of the cutting table, paused for a terrifying moment, then fell, dumping Missy, her shoulder bag, and her doll on the way. With a thud, Missy landed on the bolt of lining—right in front of the mouse hole door!

# CHAPTER 7

The soft *plock* the spool made when it hit the floor startled Mr. Max. He strode over and bent to pick it up. Missy, flat on her back on the bolt of lining, froze as she saw his hand pass near her.

"Funny," muttered Mr. Max.

His long form straightened. "Oh well," he murmured. Mr. Max put the spool down on the cutting table above Missy's head, then turned his attention to the counter at the front of the shop.

Missy was trembling. She jumped when something tugged at her shoulder, then turned and saw Flo's angry face. Missy sighed. She'd probably be confined to the house and miss the rest of the excitement.

Miles was jumpy, too. First there was Missy's narrow escape. Now Mr. Max was coming his way. Should he try to dial the telephone? Should he remain hidden and spy?

Mr. Max arrived at the counter. Miles watched him pull open the drawers.

"Aha!" Mr. Max cried. "Here are all the ladies' careful accounts! Record books, order forms, everything so neat and tidy! Very good, ladies!"

With a nasty chuckle, Mr. Max took a plastic bottle from his pocket. He unscrewed the lid and poured the bottle's contents all over the important papers in the drawers.

Smells like glue, thought Miles, hidden under the telephone receiver. Hadn't he said Max might damage things?

In his excitement, Miles poked a bit too far out of his hiding place. The telephone receiver fell off the hook with a loud clatter.

"Agh!" exclaimed Mr. Max in surprise.

He stared at the telephone. Then he spied the unlucky Miles's tail. Slowly, his hand moved out to grab it.

Miles sensed the large hand and saw a dark shadow hanging over him. He knew he would no longer be able to stay hidden. He zoomed across the counter and leaped to the floor.

"Mice!" yelled Mr. Max, clapping his hand to his head. "Are they everywhere? They're

tormenting me! I'll find their mouse holes! I'll
smoke them out!"

He leaped after Miles.

"In here, in here," came an excited whisper.
Miles looked around nervously.

"In here, Father!" Skipper yelled.

Mr. Max was almost upon them. Skipper
grabbed his father and yanked him through a
crack in the floorboard alongside the front
window. Miles realized that this must be Skipper's
hiding place.

"Aha!" yelled Mr. Max. "So this is the mouse
hole, is it?"

An evil eye squinted through the crack. An
oily mustache drooped into the opening. Furious
that his hiding place had been discovered, and
still trembling with fear over Miles's near-capture,
Skipper grabbed the end of the oily mustache
and pulled with all his might.

"Yeow!" cried Mr. Max, flying to his feet. "I'll
get you for this, you . . . you rodent! Attack *me*,
will you?"

Mr. Max lifted a bolt of fine silk and flung it
on the floor against the window ledge, blocking
the hiding place's opening. Then he banged out

of the shop, wrenching open the back door and upsetting a table of flannels on his way.

"Whew," said Miles. He and Skipper sat uncomfortably in the darkness. Miles was embarrassed at being in Skipper's hiding place, and Skipper was embarrassed to have him there.

"Well," said Miles.

Skipper cleared his throat.

"Is there another way out?" Miles asked politely.

"No," Skipper admitted.

"Well," said Miles. "That would be too heavy to move." Miles pointed at the bolt of silk over their heads. "We'd better make another way out."

Skipper sighed. He had no choice but to lead his father through his hoard of riches. There was no hope of keeping them secret now.

"The wood is thinnest at the ceiling near the other end," Skipper said.

He led Miles to the farthest end of the long, narrow space. They passed coins, bits of glass and jewelry, and a few interesting bottle caps. Miles tried his best to pretend the space was empty. At the end of the space, they stopped.

"You're right," said Miles, listening to the

hollow sound the wood of the ceiling made when he tapped on it. "The wood is thin here."

"It goes up under the display window, and there's a crack into the shop," said Skipper.

"I know the place," said Miles. "I looked at it as a possible home when I first thought of moving here. If we can make a hole, we can easily get through that crack."

After working for a while, Miles and Skipper became aware of sounds over their heads.

"Dusty," said Flo's voice.

"Through this crack, see?" said Missy's high one. "I've been under here a few times looking for Skip's hiding place."

Skipper rolled his eyes.

"They're not in here. Miles! Skipper!" said Flo.

Miles knocked on the ceiling. "Here we are!" he called.

"Here?" said Flo over their heads.

"Yes. We're making a hole," explained Miles.

"We'll help," said Flo.

In a matter of minutes, they were through. There was nothing Skipper could do to keep Flo from peering into his hiding place. Missy poked her head through, too.

"Can I come down?" she asked.

Skipper growled.

Miles cleared his throat. "This is private property," he said. "We will come up."

Missy looked eagerly at the pile of bright sparklies.

"You'll have to move this," she said.

"I know," said Skip miserably.

"Some of it's pretty," said Missy.

"I'll bring something home," said Skipper.

"You'll be generous with your family, I'm sure," said Flo. "We'll all help you move your— ah—goods."

"Oh, yes!" exclaimed Missy. "I'll help!"

"No, thank you," said Skipper, as politely as he could manage.

Miles cleared his throat.

"There are still a few hours until dawn," he said. "Let's go home and eat lunch, and rest a bit. Then, Skipper, you and I will come back here. You must not return to this place after tonight. It's too dangerous. I'll just help you load all this into bags. You can store your valuables at home until you find a new location."

There was a pause. Missy hopped a little in excitement at the thought of bags and bags of interesting things leaning against the walls of the storerooms. She wondered if Skip would let her peek into any of them.

"All right," Skipper agreed after a long moment.

"Come on, then," said Flo. "I want to get home and brew some peppermint tea."

# CHAPTER

8

Missy shut her eyes tight. She knew that Skipper and Miles would soon return with bags of treasure. She figured Skipper would bring her something, but she had to pretend to be asleep, because he hated to have his surprises spoiled.

"Not asleep yet?" said Flo from the doorway.

"I'm too excited," said Missy.

"I'm excited, too, in an unpleasant sort of way," said Flo. "I keep expecting we'll lose our home."

"Father will do something," Missy said to comfort her.

Flo came into the room and sat down on the edge of Missy's bed.

"We can't leave it all to him," she said. "He's got too much on his mind as it is. Do you know that instead of being satisfied with getting a good day's sleep and then relaxing at home tomorrow,

he and Skipper are planning to go to the inn for food as though nothing has happened? I don't mind telling you, I'm worried sick. What if Mr. Max has gotten a cat?"

Missy shivered.

"We may have to move, Missy," said Flo softly.

There was a pause.

"I don't mind," said Missy at last. "I'd hate to have to leave this home, but another would do as long as we'd all be together."

"Good girl," replied Flo fondly. "I just wish Miles would slow down, is all. He's such a worrier."

"Maybe *we* could do something," said Missy.

"What?"

"Maybe we could go to the Ladies' Circle meeting at the inn and ask for their help."

For a full minute, Flo was speechless. She was "allergic" to groups. That was one of the reasons she enjoyed living alone with her family at The Calico Scrapbag.

"Oh, Missy!" she protested.

"But everyone at the inn is in danger, too!" Missy pointed out.

"That's true," Flo admitted. "If we could get

everyone involved, they'd help us. But they have no use for The Calico Scrapbag."

"Bring them some material for dresses," Missy suggested.

"A bribe!" exclaimed Flo in a horrified voice. She was thinking of the dent such a plan would make in her storeroom.

Missy was silent while Flo thought things over.

"I suppose you're right," Flo finally admitted. "We have more than enough here. And some of those mice could certainly use more tasteful outfits."

"Besides," Missy said as she thought about digging into her own treasure trove for bundles of lace and strings of beads to offer the ladies, "they share the inn food with us. We should all share what we have."

"I feel a headache coming on," said Flo faintly. "Do you realize, Missy, that everything would change? They'd always be coming over for a bit of cotton or thread!"

"They would?" Missy gave a little hop of excitement. She wondered if there might be a mouse about her age who liked to play with dolls.

"Maybe we could have the meeting here sometimes!" Missy said eagerly. "You could serve tea and crumb cakes. You make the *best* crumb cakes."

Flo groaned.

"We could make friends!" said Missy.

"You can make friends without belonging to a club," said Flo.

"Okay," said Missy. "Could we invite them to visit anyway?"

"I guess we could ask them to drop by when they're in the shop," said Flo reluctantly.

"Oh, boy!" cried Missy.

Flo looked sharply at Missy. She had spent years carefully preserving her privacy. It hadn't occurred to her that Missy might be lonely.

"I had no idea you wanted company, Missy," she said.

"Well, sometimes," said Missy, "I wish I had someone to play with."

"Now that I think about it," said Flo, "it must be lonely for a young thing like you."

"Could we go to the inn with Miles and Skipper and drop in on *them* sometime?" asked Missy.

"I suppose."

"Oh, good!"

Flo cheered up a little. The thought of visiting someone else *was* pleasant. And she had to admit that the idea of showing off her beautiful home was pleasant, too.

"We'll do it," she declared. "The Ladies' Circle meeting is tonight. As soon as the shop is closed, we'll get up and make bundles from the storeroom. After we eat, we'll get Miles and Skipper to help us bring the bundles to the inn."

"I can't wait!"

"You may as well get up for a while," said Flo. "We'll wait for Miles and Skipper in the kitchen."

But Miles was horrified when he heard the plan.

"Too dangerous!" he announced, setting down a bag that was stuffed with goods from Skipper's hoard.

"Pooh," Flo scoffed. "A Ladies' Circle meeting *dangerous*? What nonsense! A good sleep is all you need to see the sense of it."

Missy thought that sleep was the last thing she wanted. But, like the rest of her family, she went to bed and listened from there to Misses

Finch and Finicky's alarm over finding their accounts vandalized and their shop in such a mess. In the midst of all the noise, Missy finally fell asleep. She dreamed of being chased by a cat with Mr. Max's face through a winding passage heaped with mounds of sparkling treasures.

She woke to hear Miss Finch's voice, clear and loud, saying: "With the police driving by every hour tonight, there should be no further disturbance from our intruder. He's a coward and a bully, that's what he is!"

Miss Finicky gasped.

"Do you know who is causing us so much worry?" she asked.

"I have my theory!" said Miss Finch darkly.

There was the sound of the door opening, and a key in the lock. The door closed. Then there was a new sound, a loud metallic noise. Must be a new kind of lock, thought Missy.

She rolled out of bed, pulled her covers up quickly, and hurried into the kitchen. There Flo was talking to Miles as she filled two sacks with lengths of cloth.

"There," said Flo briskly, patting the bulging sacks. "That will do for a start."

"Who will watch the shop," demanded Miles, "if you go to meetings and we go for food?"

There was a short silence. Miles and Flo glared at each other.

"You could go for food tomorrow night," suggested Missy.

"What about the cat?" roared Miles.

Missy lowered her head. Miles never yelled. Flo came and put a hand on Missy's shoulder.

"You could check it out for us first," said Flo quietly. "You could smell a cat right off. And after you show us where the meeting is, you and Skipper could watch the shop. We have to try it, Miles. We need help."

"I hate asking for help," said Miles.

"I know," said Flo. "But we're all in a lot of trouble. We should band together now."

Miles scowled.

"All right," he said. "We'll try it. You get ready while I go check on the inn."

Missy ran back to her room. She chose her prettiest trims to add to Flo's sacks and filled her shoulder bag with beads. She put on her new lavender dress. Then she went back to the kitchen and sat down next to Skipper at the table.

"Why do *you* look so glum?" she asked. "*I* think this is exciting!"

"I have to find a new hiding place," said Skipper. "One Father doesn't know about. And one that will be hard to find. If mice from the inn come swarming in here, nothing will be safe!"

"Oh, pooh," said Missy unsympathetically.

She decided that now was not a good time to ask Skip what he'd brought her from his treasures. She gave a short sigh and waited impatiently for Miles's return.

Flo made Skipper tell her over and over again how to get from the inn kitchen to all the emergency exits.

"I know the inn pretty well, of course," she explained to Missy, "but it's been years since I've been there, and things have changed."

Missy listened intently. Her heart was beating as fast as she could ever remember it beating. She was going to the inn tonight! She was going to meet some other mice!

They all fell silent when they heard Miles in the passageway. He came into the kitchen, looking tired and worried.

"No cats yet," he reported. "The kitchen's quiet."

"Good," said Flo. "Missy, get ready."

Missy hurried off. She scrubbed her face until it shone and arranged a small, green bow behind her ear. Then she grabbed up her shoulder bag and ran to join Skipper and Flo. Skipper had a double load, a sack and his backpack. Miles was going to stand guard in the shop.

"Watch out for rat poison," warned Flo as she kissed Miles good-bye.

"Watch out for cats and humans," returned Miles. He kissed Missy on the cheek. "Stay close to your mother."

Missy nodded impatiently. She hurried after Skipper, pretending to be a great explorer traveling to foreign lands.

# CHAPTER

9

Missy had been outside before, as far as the driveway, but never to the inn. She followed Skipper and Flo across the gravel, dodging rocks and boulders and pieces of glass. The grass at the other side was shoulder-high on her, and it parted reluctantly as she passed through it behind Flo. The grass was like an upside-down curtain of stiff satin ribbon and smelled spicy-sweet. Missy sneezed from the dust Flo kicked up.

"Shh!" whispered Flo sharply.

"It tickles," giggled Missy.

"*Shhhhh*, I said!" whispered Flo. "We're almost there."

"Here," whispered Skipper as they reached the crack next to the inn's outside faucet. "Put your bags in first, then squeeze yourselves through. I'll boost you up."

He helped Flo in, then pushed Missy up. She

came through the crack with a jerk and fell a few inches to a wooden ledge.

"Watch out for the drop," whispered Skipper as he eased himself in behind her.

Missy glared at him. She followed him and Flo along the passageway. She brushed against a hot pipe and yelped. A glance from Skipper silenced her. It seemed forever until the darkness was broken by light from the hole behind the refrigerator.

"This is the kitchen, Missy," whispered Skipper. "Farther up the passageway is the back of the corner cupboard—the Squealers' home. Meeting's there tonight. There's a trap, but you can easily get around it."

Flo took a long, deep breath. The Squealers weren't her favorites, and Fatty Squealer had started this whole cat scare. Still, they'd come this far.

"Let's go," she whispered.

Missy swallowed a few times. She patted her ear bow for reassurance. Meeting other mice sounded like fun at home, but actually doing it made her heart rise to her throat.

The trap was easy to slide by, just as Skipper

had promised. Flo glanced at it matter-of-factly and went calmly past, but Missy stared at its horrible metal spring. She inched past it sideways, half-expecting it to lunge at her. The peanut butter on it smelled wonderful.

The passageway to the Squealers' home was littered and dusty. Flo's nose twitched in distaste. There were even paper scraps in front of the mouse hole door.

"Here we are," said Skipper. "I'll meet you behind the refrigerator after lunch."

He winked at Missy and disappeared into the dark passage.

Missy nervously smoothed her dress. She clutched the strap of the sack, and Flo hoisted her own sack up again.

"Well, Miss," she said. Her voice trembled a little. "No matter what happens tonight, be polite. Remember all the manners I've taught you. Don't speak until you're spoken to, say thank you, and don't ask for food."

Missy nodded.

Flo took a deep breath. "Now," she said.

She knocked on the Squealers' door. It opened to reveal a fat fuzzball of a mouse, wearing an orange dress, which had obviously once been a linen tablecloth, and a huge white apron. Her face expressed pure amazement.

"Why, Floretta Calico!" she exclaimed.

Missy blinked. She'd had no idea her mother's name was Floretta.

"Hello, Letitia," said Flo calmly. "I knew there was a meeting tonight, so I brought over some fabric from the Scrapbag. I hope we're not intruding."

"Why, no, for heaven's sake. You come right on in," said Letitia Squealer. "This your girl?"

"Yes, this is Missy," said Flo, poking Missy in the ribs.

"How do you do," said Missy faintly.

"Why, she's real sweet," said Mrs. Squealer. "Come into the parlor and make yourselves at home. I'll call my Gladys. She's about your Missy's age. They can get to know each other."

Flo and Missy followed their hostess into a room that was brightly lit and very hot, thanks to many lighted candle ends in jar lids.

"Here's Floretta Calico and her Missy," announced Mrs. Squealer with the air of a magician producing a rabbit. "You remember everyone, Flo: Annie Gray, Blanche Longtail, and Carrie Littlemouse. Amber Twitch should be along soon. She has two new babies to bed down first."

"How nice!" exclaimed Flo. "There's some good pieces of flannel in my bags she could use. I've been meaning to bring you some fabric all along. Truth is, I haven't been feeling very well since Missy was born."

Missy raised her eyebrows. Mother hadn't been sick in her entire life.

"You go play with Gladys," hissed Flo, "and make sure you're nice to her! I'll take care of this."

Missy smiled shyly at Gladys Squealer, a happy-looking creature with enormous eyes.

"I've got some beads in my bag," Missy said. "Want some?"

Gladys grabbed Missy's sleeve.

"Come to my room and show me," she suggested.

Missy nodded to the ladies, but no one noticed. They were all very busy going through Flo's pile of fabric, exclaiming over lengths of cotton prints and pieces of real silk. Mother has really risen to the

occasion, thought Missy with admiration as she slipped down the narrow hall after Gladys.

"Here's my room," said Gladys.

"It's nice," said Missy, looking at the menu-covered walls.

"You live in The Calico Scrapbag, don't you?" said Gladys. "My mother says your mother thinks she's too good for us."

She watched Missy from under long lashes.

Uh-oh. Missy took a deep breath.

"I don't think that's it," she said carefully. "She thinks everyone got mad at her when she moved to The Calico Scrapbag, and she's very proud. She didn't want to come back without being invited. But I think she wanted to." Missy crossed her fingers behind her back. "I think she was just waiting around for a reason."

"Oh, okay," said Gladys cheerfully. "Then you can come visit."

"And you can come visit me," said Missy happily. "I know good places to get lace and beads and stuff. Look!"

Missy turned her shoulder bag upside down. Gladys gasped as beads and sequins rolled across the floor.

"They're beautiful!" she cried, picking up a clear red bead.

"You can have them," said Missy, happy to see she'd pleased her new friend.

"I can give you something, too," said Gladys.

She pulled a Jell-O box out from under her bed, puffing a little with exertion. She opened the box and produced a colorful collection of bright pictures on cardboard.

"What are they?" asked Missy, reaching out for one that showed a yellow butterfly.

"Matchbook covers," said Gladys. "My father brings them home when the matches are used up. You can read them or use them for scrapbooks."

"Read?" breathed Missy. "You can *read*?"

"Sure," said Gladys. "Mama and I learned from cookbooks. The cook reads them out loud a lot. It's catching."

"Will you teach me?" asked Missy eagerly.

"Okay," Gladys agreed.

"Wow!" cried Missy.

She and Gladys sat on the floor, examining the matchbook covers and discussing which were better, round beads or long ones.

After a while, Mrs. Squealer came in, carrying a tray laden with good-smelling food.

"Here you are," she said. "Gladys, bring the tray back to the kitchen when you're done. Your mother has been real generous, Missy."

Missy smiled and sniffed the tray of warm food hungrily.

"Hope you like baked potato," said Mrs. Squealer.

"I've never had it," said Missy. "It smells *wonderful*!"

Mrs. Squealer left, looking pleased. Missy accepted the helping Gladys offered her. So *that* was baked potato, and *that* was melted cheese! The most Flo could manage by way of hot food was soup or tea heated on the hot water pipe.

"How'd your mom cook this?" asked Missy, her mouth full of baked potato.

"Daddy built a stove out of tin cans and candles when Mama learned how to read cookbooks," replied Gladys.

Missy sighed. What luxury!

When Flo called that it was time to go home, Missy accepted two matchbooks—one with a shiny gold cover, for Skip, and one with a lovely mountain scene on it, which she planned to use as a lace scrapbook. She thought of a hundred more things to tell Gladys, and they both promised to visit. Then Flo whisked her out the door.

"It was a lovely meeting," said Flo. "We *did* get a lot accomplished, Letitia. When all this business has died down, you'll have to come visit us at the shop."

"We'll attend to Max," said Mrs. Squealer, looking like an avenging angel. "And thank you for the fabric. 'Bye, Missy."

"Good-bye, Mrs. Squealer," said Missy. "Thank you for lunch. You're a wonderful cook. Bring Gladys to visit me!" she called as Flo pushed her into the passageway.

"Hush, said Flo, digging her in the ribs. "We're behind the kitchen!"

Missy was quiet until they'd reached a place a few feet behind the refrigerator.

"How was the meeting?" she asked curiously.

"Very satisfactory," said Flo smugly. "After seeing the fabric I'd brought, the ladies decided that they didn't want The Calico Scrapbag turned into a parking lot. That's what Mr. Max wants to do—Fatty Squealer heard him say so. And they seem to have a great many complaints about Mr. Max. He spends so much of the day yelling that they can't sleep. He's also stingy about food. Everyone wants him out. The cook can take over—he's a nice, nearsighted man. I'll tell you more later. I see Skipper coming."

# CHAPTER 10

The Calicos had a picnic on the cutting table with the food Mrs. Squealer had wrapped in tin foil and sent back with Flo. Sheltered by a row of pincushions, they munched happily on the still-warm food while Flo outlined her session with the Ladies' Circle.

"We have allies," she began grandly. "After I told the ladies about the trouble Max is causing in the shop, they told me how disagreeable he is to live with at the inn. They were eager to plan a way to rid themselves of him."

"Hear, hear!" said Skipper.

"What about the cat?" asked Miles.

"Of course, we are *all* worried about the cat," said Flo. "Fortunately, the cook hates cats. He's all for traps and poison, which are dangerous and unpleasant, but we could learn to live with them. The thing to do is to get rid of Max altogether."

Flo paused. "We've even planned how to do it!"

"Now, that's what I call a good evening's work!" exclaimed Miles.

"Mr. Max is not in town tonight," continued Flo. "He attends an innkeeper's convention in New York City on the second Wednesday of every month. But we'll have to do something soon. He's been storing gallons of gasoline in the basement—eight of them. Blanche Longtail told me."

"I know," said Miles with a nod. "I saw them earlier."

"Gasoline," said Missy weakly. "Isn't that something you can use to start fires?"

"Yes, Missy," said Miles.

"Oh," said Missy.

"So Max must be planning to burn down The Calico Scrapbag," continued Flo. "But not tonight, because he's in New York. So," Flo took a deep breath, "everyone is coming here tomorrow night. To stop him. And after he's caught, the shop will be safe and the cook will become the new manager of the inn, and there won't be any cats!"

Flo waited triumphantly for applause.

"How?" asked Miles.

"How what?"

"How will we stop him?"

"Oh," said Flo. "I have no idea. But we'll have to do *something*, or I brought all my best fabric to the Ladies' Circle meeting for nothing!"

Miles rubbed his ears.

"Well," he said. "I'd best go talk to the fellows. We'll think of something."

There was a long silence. Missy had trouble swallowing her mouthful of potato. What could mice do against the evil Mr. Max?

"Caps," said Skipper quietly.

"What?"

"Caps," Skipper repeated. "You drop something heavy on them, like stones, and they bang."

"They bang?" said Flo blankly.

"Explode," said Skipper. "Make noise."

"Caps," said Miles thoughtfully.

Missy had an idea. She took a sharp breath and sat up straight.

"Beads!" she said excitedly.

"Beads?" chorused Miles and Flo.

"Yes!" said Missy. "Lots of them, all over the floor! He'll trip!"

"Why, I believe he would," agreed Miles, looking from Missy to Skip in amazement.

"And marbles," said Skip. "Those are even bigger. I have some in my new hiding place," he added. "Where I also have a roll of caps."

"Pincushions," said Missy. "With lots of needles."

"Tapestry thread spread between all the counters," said Skip. "He'd trip, for sure."

"Onto the pincushions," said Missy, giggling.

Miles and Flo sat spellbound.

"What happens when we get him down?" asked Miles carefully. "What will we do with him then?"

"Throw a piece of cloth over his head," said Missy. "I do that when I'm playing ghost. You can't see a thing."

"There'll be enough mice to hold him down, Miles!" said Flo, entering into the spirit of the thing.

"But he's big, Flo, a human being!" protested Miles. "We could keep him down for a moment or two, but he could get up any time."

They sagged. It had looked so hopeful. Then Skipper spoke up.

"I know where the alarm button is," he said.

"What's an alarm button?" demanded Missy.

"Miss Finch had an alarm system installed after the shop was broken into the other night," said Skip. "The doors are hooked up to it, and there's a button on the floor behind the front counter. When Mr. Max comes in, all we have to do is stop him until the police arrive."

"Why not push the button as soon as Mr. Max comes in?" Missy asked.

"He'd just turn and run," said Skip. "The trick is to get him down first. It will take a little organization," he continued. "We'll have to have the beads and marbles and pincushions and other weapons ready when he comes in."

"Once the police get here, we'll all have to disappear," Missy said. "As long as there aren't any mice in sight, no one will believe Mr. Max when he says mice were everywhere."

"Well," said Miles, "let's call a general meeting at the inn to get things organized."

"Missy and I will prepare for the siege," announced Flo.

"And gather the beads and pincushions," said Missy. "And the cloth for his head."

"Maybe you'd better stay here, Skipper," said Miles, "and take care of the, uh, caps and marbles."

"I'll put everything where it's easy to get to," Skipper said.

"But where it won't be found by Misses Finch and Finicky when they open," warned Miles.

"I think I've done a rather good job of hiding things in the past," said Skipper. He seemed rather hurt.

"True. Sorry," said Miles.

"I'll come to the inn when I'm done and tell you where the stockpiles will be," said Skipper.

"Good thinking," said Miles.

"Come on, Miss," said Flo. "We have to lay in a supply of food for after the fighting."

And so the Calicos went off to prepare for the coming battle.

# CHAPTER

11

There never had been a night such as this. For the first time in memory, fifty mice were gathered together against a human being, ready for battle and determined to win. It was the Day of the Mouse, and would be so remembered in mouse history for all time to come.

Skipper had done his job well. The night before, he had hidden marbles, beads, and pincushions with needles in them all around the shop. He had done it so well that Misses Finch and Finicky had noticed nothing extraordinary except the absence of twenty-four bags of beads and thirty-six cards of needles. This they noted down as a mistake in inventory.

An hour after the shop closed, in the shelter of the early autumn darkness, Skipper and Miles had spent an exhausting hour stretching tapestry yarn from one counter to another in six different places where it might trip an unsuspecting Max. Twenty-five pincushions, fat with needles, squatted here and there, waiting to be fallen upon. After all the mice from the inn had arrived, Miles and Skip had assigned pairs of them to the pincushions and to the two stockpiles of beads and marbles. Now these mice stood guard, ready to roll the weapons out at the sound of someone breaking in.

A roll of caps was spread out on the shelf above the entrance to the Calicos' home. Missy and Flo were among the mice who were lined up along the tops of the bolts of cloth above the caps. In front of each mouse were some hefty stones, hauled in with great effort from the driveway. At the right moment, the mice were prepared to push the stones over the edges of the bolts onto the caps below. It was hoped that the ensuing explosions would add to Mr. Max's fear and confusion and keep him from rising after he had tripped over the yarn or fallen on the beads and marbles.

A brave group of volunteers, led by Miles, had pulled a large piece of lightweight cotton from a table. This piece of cotton was now lying

underneath the cutting table, where Miles and five other brave mice were ready to run it to the location of Mr. Max's head once he was on the floor. Leggy Longtail was actually willing to run across Mr. Max's face with his end, if necessary. And, most important of all, Skipper and Fatty Squealer were stationed at the alarm button, prepared to set it off.

Outside the shop, darkness fell. Inside the shop, all was still. Each mouse waited at his or her post with a pounding heart. Each knew how important it was to succeed. Each feared the thought of injury. A human could so easily knock a mouse away with his hand, or, worse, step on a mouse with his enormous feet.

Up in the cap line, Missy stood behind her biggest stone, ready to push with all her might. It took every bit of her concentration just to keep still. She could hear the breathing of the mice to either side of her. She wished Gladys was beside her, but Gladys was inside the Calicos' home, babysitting the smallest mice, including Amber Twitch's tiny twins. Missy craned to catch a glimpse of the marble stockpile and the two mice guarding it. She knew that, like her, they were listening for the slightest sound that might indicate Mr. Max's arrival. Missy wanted him to come, yet she dreaded his arrival. She stifled a sigh. It was the waiting she couldn't stand.

To get her mind off the question of whether Mr. Max would show up at all, Missy began to imagine how he would break in. She wondered if he knew the doors were hooked up to an alarm system. She expected that he would enter by the back window again. If so, he would trip over the tapestry yarn that was stretched between the cutting table and the button display rack. If he did trip, he would sprawl within inches of the mice guarding the marbles. Their job was to roll the beads and marbles out while Max was falling. Just thinking of it made Missy want to roll some noisy beads around now and break the silence.

After two hours of motionless waiting, there came a faint sound of footsteps on gravel. Missy felt Mrs. Squealer straighten next to her, and she heard Flo draw in her breath. She knew all the other mice in the shop were holding their breath, too. She could hear the distant sound of a tiny mouse squeaking.

*Clunk. Scrape.* Then Missy heard the sound of

splintering wood. Mr. Max had jimmied the window frame and was now pushing up the window. Every nerve in Missy's body tingled. Her tail stood at attention.

The back window now stood open. Into the patch of pale light the moon cast on the floor, Missy saw a gigantic black shadow loom. The shadow moved, and she heard ominous clanks as some large metal objects were lifted into the shop. A faint but unmistakable odor of gasoline scented the air. The shadow moved again. Someone was pulling himself into the shop! The shadow closed the window and pulled the curtains across it. All was darkness once again.

There was the scrape of tin on wood and a *glug, glug, glug.* Gasoline! Mr. Max had begun to pour gasoline out already! The mice on the floor were in danger. Something must be done!

In her excitement, Missy pushed the stone she was leaning against, and it set off a cap. *Bang!*

"Oh, *do* something, *do* something!" Flo cried, dropping several rocks at once. Two more caps exploded.

"What's that!" exclaimed Mr. Max.

Miles jumped into the aisle, making as much

noise as possible. He hoped to lure Mr. Max toward the center of the shop. Skipper pulled desperately at a heavy book on the bottom shelf of the front counter. It toppled to the floor with a loud *clump*.

Mr. Max swore. He took a step forward and caught sight of Miles in the pale light from the front window.

"Mice, again!" he cursed. "I'll get you this time!"

Mr. Max took a step toward Miles, tripped over a length of tapestry yarn, and tumbled toward the floor.

*"Now!"* yelled Miles.

From all directions came beads and marbles, rolling toward the falling Max and making a racket as loud as cannonballs to Missy's frightened ears.

*"Yeow!"* yelled the villain.

Unable to regain his balance, he fell heavily to the floor. His nose landed smack against a pincushion bristling with needles.

"Now, now, now!" cried Flo. The mice in the cap line hurled down stones, setting up exclamation-point explosions. When Missy had trouble pushing a particularly sharp stone forward, Mrs. Squealer came to her aid.

Down on the floor, brave mice ran toward the prone Max, pulling the length of cotton fabric behind them. The cloth billowed over Max's head. The mice gathered around him to pull the cloth tight. More mice armed with tapestry needles rushed up to the squirming figure. They jabbed at his hands as he struggled to rise.

"Now!" cried Skip.

Together, he and Fatty Squealer pounced on the alarm button. The Calico Scrapbag began to ring with the noise of an electric bell. An angry red light flashed on and off.

Then began a battle the mice would remember all their lives. They would relive it for their great-grandchildren, and the story would be passed down as a legend from generation to generation. While the red light flashed on and off, throwing a glare of danger and fear onto the scene, the band of fifty mice grimly battled a human being for life and home.

They stuck needles into Max's hands. They climbed atop shelves of fabric and pushed bolts

of cloth down on him. They fought not only with a strong, struggling human, but with gasoline, which ran in rivers between the floorboards. Two brave mice had to be dragged away from the battlefield when they fainted from the fumes. Mr. Max sent Skipper flying against a counter, breaking two of his legs. Miles and Fatty Squealer carried Skipper to safety. Just as the villain was getting to his feet, cursing at the needles in his hands and striking out at the mice around him, there came the wonderful sound of a police siren.

Immediately, the mice retreated to the Calicos' home. They left behind the flashing red light, the alarm bell, and a scene of great disorder. They disappeared into the mouse hole at the exact moment the front door broke open and a stern voice ordered:

"*Stop!* In the name of the Law!"

Miles and Fatty and the wounded Skipper huddled in the entrance to the mouse hole with Missy and Gladys, who each held a tiny baby mouse. They watched as the police hurried the protesting Max away.

"It was mice!" Mr. Max stuttered. "I tried to stop them, but they were everywhere. Everywhere!"

"Yes, yes," said one of the policemen patiently.

"I'm telling you the truth!" cried Max.

The policeman shook his head and took his prisoner out to the waiting squad car.

The mice were too tired and worried about the wounded to be able to celebrate their victory. But they couldn't rest. As long as gasoline was in the shop, The Calico Scrapbag was in danger of burning. As the fire department arrived to see to the shop's safety, the mice crept swiftly out the back mouse hole, streaked across the driveway, and marched through the grass, into The Gray Cat Inn, carrying their wounded. No one saw them in the flurry of police cars, TV crews, and fire trucks.

The Calicos settled into the Squealers' home in back of the corner cupboard. Missy was grateful to climb into Gladys's big bed. She felt very sorry for Skip, whose legs had been set in casts of matchsticks and wire, and who was groaning with pain.

"My poor bother," she whispered to Gladys.

"He's so brave!" sighed Gladys.

"I keep hearing that bell," whispered Missy,

"all loud and screaming."

"We're safe now," Gladys reassured Missy, patting her arm. "Your brother will be fine, and your home's safe, too. You'll see!"

Missy settled into her pillows and listened to the murmur of the grown-ups talking. Morning came before she finally closed her eyes. As she drifted off to sleep, the nightmare sound of the bell faded, leaving behind it only the glow of victory.

# Epilogue

In about a week or so, the shop returned to normal, and the Calicos moved back home. Skipper spent two miserable months in casts of matchsticks and wire. For the rest of his life, he walked with a limp, but he became legendary as the general who had planned the campaign of the Day of the Mouse. Miles was bursting with pride. Flo became a community leader and was happy to welcome visitors to her home. Missy had a host of friends. In time she became known for her work for better housing conditions for mice everywhere. The Calicos traveled widely, crossing dangerous driveways and vacationing in unexplored kitchens and the storerooms of enormous supermarkets. But they always returned home to The Calico Scrapbag, where, with Misses Finch and Finicky, they live to this day.